Savage Conversations

Savage Conversations

LEANNE HOWE

COFFEE HOUSE PRESS

Minneapolis

2019

Coffee House Press books are available to the trade through our primary dis-
tributor, Consortium Book Sales & Distribution, cbsd.com or (800) 283-3572.
For personal orders, catalogs, or other information, write to info@coffeehouse
press.org.

Coffee House Press is a nonprofit literary publishing house. Support from
private foundations, corporate giving programs, government programs, and
generous individuals helps make the publication of our books possible. We
gratefully acknowledge their support in detail in the back of this book.

LIBRARY OF CONGRESS CATALOGING-IN-PUBLICATION DATA

Names: Howe, LeAnne, author.
Title: Savage conversations / LeAnne Howe ; with an introduction by
    Susan Power.
Description: Minneapolis : Coffee House Press, 2019.
Identifiers: LCCN 2018027629 (print) | LCCN 2018028476 (ebook) |
    ISBN 9781566895408 | ISBN 9781566895316 (trade pbk.)
Subjects: LCSH: Lincoln, Mary Todd, 1818–1882—Fiction. | Indians of North
    America—Fiction. | United States—History—1849–1877—Fiction.
    GSAFD: Historical fiction.
Classification: LCC PS3608.O95 (ebook) | LCC PS3608.O95 S28 2019 (print) |
    DDC 813/.6—dc23
LC record available at https://lccn.loc.gov/2018027629

ACKNOWLEDGMENTS

Excerpts from *Savage Conversations* have appeared in
World Literature Today and on Literary Hub.

For the enduring and courageous spirit
of the Dakota people

INTRODUCTION

Susan Power

LeAnne Howe was living and teaching in Illinois in 2008 as the state was on the cusp of celebrating Abraham Lincoln's two hundredth birthday the following year. As scholars delved into well-traveled Lincoln archives in search of fresh perspectives on old stories, LeAnne was intrigued by all the fuss.

Being Native American in this country means often having a very different take on American history and historic figures generally accepted as national heroes. Just because they're your heroes doesn't make them automatically ours, since what benefited non-Native settlers was often dangerously harmful to indigenous communities. So from the very outset of her investigation, LeAnne's analysis of Lincoln history was brilliantly original, innovative, and fascinating. She drew conclusions that were wildly different from those that came before, yet she made a good case for her astonishing insights. I was honored to take the journey with her, hear what new theories leaped to mind while she sorted through old papers and familiar stories. As she read biographies, letters, and diaries, she became increasingly interested in the former first lady, Mary Todd Lincoln. Perhaps because Mary's own story is compelling, perhaps because LeAnne is Choctaw—a tribal nation following matrilineal kinship ties that invest Choctaw women with enormous political power—LeAnne focused on this troubled woman who was the mother of a nation while its territories were awash in the blood of a vicious civil war. And what she thought of Mary Todd Lincoln was riveting.

LeAnne phoned me one day to share an exciting revelation she'd had as she tracked the various illnesses of the Lincolns' four children, only one of whom survived to full adulthood. She said the boys seemed to revive when they were in the care of people other than their mother, but would often fail again soon after Mary returned to nurse them, dose them. LeAnne suspected Mary Todd Lincoln might have suffered from Munchausen syndrome by proxy. I gasped at her words, how unexpected yet profoundly sensible they were given what I knew of Mary and her desperate need for attention—first from her father, as a worshipful daughter having to compete with fifteen siblings, and then from her husband, with his brutal schedule and professional obligations. While Mary absolutely supported her husband in his political ambitions, she was often left alone to manage their affairs. Munchausen syndrome by proxy is a rare disorder whereby a parent or caregiver seeks the sympathetic attention of others by exaggerating the symptoms of their children, or inventing symptoms, or making the children ill, sometimes fatally. LeAnne couldn't be positive of this diagnosis, but as her version of Mary Todd Lincoln began to develop, this possibility informed the world of *Savage Conversations*.

Through LeAnne's research I learned that after the assassination of President Lincoln, Mary's mental health continued to decline, and by the 1870s, she was complaining to her doctor of nightly visits from a violent "Indian," who she said scalped her, cut bones from her cheeks, and made slits in her eyelids, sewing them open. *Who was this "Indian"?* LeAnne wondered. *Why did he haunt Mary's imagination?* Another intuitive leap told her he was Dakota, one of the thirty-eight Dakota men hanged in a mass killing the day after Christmas in 1862. Mary's husband signed the order for their execution. LeAnne told me this news in a whisper, respectful, tactful, aware that these murdered men were members of my own tribal nation, my relatives, mindful that I grew up hearing stories of all the damage that was done to my people by President Lincoln, his administration, his troops and generals. The terrible impact he had on the Dakota nation is usually omitted in Lincoln biographies and films. The president lives on through worshipful legends and scholarship, while Dakota people and their stories are overlooked, ignored by mainstream society. LeAnne's character Savage Indian asks Mary, "Who says Abe is dead?" I shivered at the question, realizing that Abe will never be dead, not while his story lives on. And were it not for LeAnne's discovery of the Dakota character whose voice she resurrects from a mass grave, and for the dedicated work of Dakota writers and educators, his would be the ultimate death—an erasure of his experience.

When I first heard LeAnne perform excerpts of *Savage Conversations,* I was awed by the power of her dialogue. Her emphatic words singed my breath. With a few deft lines she introduced the dark history I'd grown up hearing from my Dakota mother and grandmother, passed down from my great-great-grandfather, Chief Mahto Nunpa (Two Bear). He was living in Dakota Territory in 1862 but had heard of the hard times our relatives were suffering in Minnesota. They were going hungry, their children starving, yet money owed to them by treaty was delayed, and the trader whose store carried all the supplies the Dakota needed to survive refused to extend them credit. He offered them nothing but the most cruel words: "If they are hungry, let them eat grass or dung." Our relatives rose up in their misery and killed white settlers who feasted off our territory like greedy locusts, refusing to honor treaty agreements they said they would never break. In retaliation for the violence in Minnesota, Northern generals declared war on all Dakota people, whether they were part of the desperate uprising or not. Ultimately hundreds of Dakota people were massacred, including many members of Two Bear's village. And on a startlingly beautiful morning in 1862, thirty-eight Dakota men passed through a mob of four thousand jeering white people. They ascended with great dignity a scaffold that was built for the purpose of hanging them simultaneously. After the order was given to release the platform, many took a long time to die. One man's rope broke and he fell to the ground. A new rope was summoned in order to hang him again. Once all the Dakota were gone, a cheer burst from the crowd. This is the terrible story I hear LeAnne's Savage Indian reference in his remarks, this man whose name is lost to Mary, who sees him as nothing more than a caricature dreamed up in her nightmares.

LeAnne was well into writing an early draft of *Savage Conversations* when a new character arrived, seemingly from nowhere: The Rope. The Rope cannot contain his anger, his violent work; he "seethes." He appears as a noose. He tells us, "I come when I'm called," and "This is how I make brothers and sisters." He begins to fashion another noose with his hands, creating relatives, his brothers and sisters. The words sound so innocent, but the action tells all: as he winds more rope into another noose, I can't help thinking of all the rope that in human hands has viciously strung up so many people of color—the horrific tradition of lynching in America. The Rope is a merciless truth-teller. The Rope's appearance in LeAnne's project confirmed for me that this was sacred work. To underscore this conclusion I soon learned from LeAnne that the same week The Rope manifested in her text, one of the original nooses used in the mass execution of 1862 had been unearthed at Fort Snelling in Minnesota. The instrument of Savage Indian's death had been preserved as a curiosity, then was hidden for countless years, only to reemerge as LeAnne's story developed on the page.

LeAnne Howe has been my favorite writer since I first came across her work in the late 1980s. She is always a step ahead of nearly everyone else's ideas. She is fearless. Her characters break my heart and then mend it. Her vision is utterly unique. Her Savage Indian character tells Mary, whose eyes he has skewered open to make her look at everything she never wanted to see: "With your eyes sewn open you still see nothing." Mary isn't able to see beyond the madness that will ultimately claim her, but I am the grateful beneficiary of LeAnne's perceptive vision in this book that burns through accepted stories like fire, calling me to look harder. We create the world and unmake it with our stories. There are times when only imagination can save us.

Savage Conversations

THE STORY

President Abraham Lincoln gave the order to execute thirty-eight Dakota Indians in Mankato, Minnesota, for their actions in the Dakota War against white settlers who had first stolen their lands, then their rations, and raped their women. At 10 a.m. on December 26, 1862, the synchronized hanging of thirty-eight Dakota was, and continues to be, the largest mass execution in United States history. Four thousand settlers attended the execution. After the mass burial, the bodies of the American Indians were dug up by a local doctor and used as medical cadavers.

Fast-forward eleven years to November 1873. Dr. Willis Danforth of Illinois treats Mary Todd Lincoln for "nervous derangement and fever in her head." He notes peculiar symptoms. Nightly, Mrs. Lincoln claims, someone lifts her scalp and replaces it by dawn, sometimes cutting a bone out of her cheek. She attributes the fiendish work inside her head to an Indian spirit. "The Indian," she says, "slits my eyelids and sews them open, always removing the wires by dawn's first light."[1]

Mrs. Lincoln's nervous condition becomes legendary much to the dismay of her only surviving son, Robert Lincoln. In

---

1. Mark E. Neely Jr. and R. Gerald McMurtry, *The Insanity File: The Case of Mary Todd Lincoln* (Carbondale, IL: Southern Illinois University Press, 1986), 11.

May 1875, Mary Todd Lincoln goes on trial in Chicago for insanity. Judge Marion Wallace presides. Robert testifies against his mother. The jury deliberates for ten minutes before bringing in a verdict. They recommend that she be placed in an asylum. Robert Lincoln escorts Mary Todd Lincoln to Bellevue Place Sanitarium on Jefferson Street in Batavia, Illinois. Once there, she's ensconced in a private residence. Mary Todd Lincoln continues to have visions that an American Indian spirit enters her room and tortures her.

THE CHARACTERS

MARY TODD LINCOLN. Wife of slain President Abraham Lincoln. She wears a wrinkled dress with Tad Lincoln's pistol hidden in the pocket. At night she refuses to remove the tattered nightdress and undergarments that she's worn for months. Her hair is disheveled.

SAVAGE INDIAN. One of the thirty-eight Dakota men hanged the day after Christmas, 1862, in Mankato, Minnesota. He sits in a chair in a dark corner of her room. His hair is dark brown and shoulder length. He wears a black vigilante town coat, the one he was hanged in. The coat droops open because the hangman's wife cut off the buttons to sew onto her new frock.

THE ROPE. Both a man *and* the image of a hangman's noose used in the largest mass execution in United States history. The Rope eavesdrops on Mary and Savage Indian's conversations. He sometimes twirls around the room like a dancer.

Scene 1

They Speak of Dreams

APOCRYPHA

June 1875

Bellevue Place Sanitarium, 333 S. Jefferson Street,
Batavia, Illinois

MARY TODD LINCOLN

Before you can think, you forget and then remember
A dress of blood, gloves I refuse to wash.
Ever.

What is it to a wild Indian? *The president is shot.*
Fool, I was his all-in-all, his Molly, his child-wife and
mother, his puss.

SAVAGE INDIAN
Thoughtfully.
Well . . . he called me puss, too.

CATAFALQUE

June 1875

Bellevue Place Sanitarium, 333 S. Jefferson Street,
Batavia, Illinois

*Midnight, Mary's bedroom. The underarms of her nightdress are
badly soiled. Her small feet are swollen, the skin paper-thin. She
speaks to Mr. Lincoln as if he's in her room.*

*Savage Indian has a small box on his lap filled with her jewelry.
He fingers each piece and finally fastens a pearl necklace around
his neck.*

MARY TODD LINCOLN

Nightly, I examine our ruined heads in my hand mirror:
yours and mine.
Our eyes dangle like dull grapes on a broken vine. Is it the
candlelight?

SAVAGE INDIAN
Watches her with menacing eyes but does not move.

MARY TODD LINCOLN

I touch the blemish on your face, finger your blood-stained
shirt; a drop of spittle has escaped your tight lips, your bare
feet clammy as fish, all there, and here; I kiss the mirror,
beg you to wake, fight to catch your attention through
some mad, theatrical gesture, remember? My bed, always
a catafalque to you: oh let fly my flesh, hair, and eyelash;

pay the Nightjar who regularly serenades and, like us,
steals the milk of goats.

Here, at last, I'll tell it all: I did wish you dead, sir, eight
thousand thirty-nine times for all the days you ran
sideways from our home, whistling a Nightjar's tune. Pay
them all now, sir, before dawn's light.

SAVAGE INDIAN
Reads aloud the inscription of her wedding ring.
Love Is Eternal.

CATAFALQUE II

June 1875

Bellevue Place Sanitarium, 333 S. Jefferson Street,
Batavia, Illinois

*Mary Todd Lincoln and Savage Indian pace around the room
like amateur boxers.*

MARY TODD LINCOLN

Arriving nightly without invitation,
You make my room a ceremony as
Nightjars sing, wing-clap, chirr their song,
Inhibited at dawn by God's will, like we are.

When shall I tell them the truth?
Where shall I keep the truth?
Under my frayed petticoat,
It will not flower now.

She fingers a small picture of Abraham Lincoln on her bureau.

There is no need to wait for tea: I confess,
Though you coveted another, I longed for
The pleasure of your coarse skin,
Money to spend, kid gloves, chiffon and satin
Ball gowns with lavish trains properly hemmed.
Doomed children.

Tonight, let us hoist the catafalque over a new grave.
Hold my hands above the dank earth as the Nightjars
serenade.

Oh what a great heart-smasher you are, Mr. Lincoln.
Adieu, my confessor, my all-in-all, lover, protector, ghost
husband.

Turns to Savage Indian.

Wishing for nothing, not even breath,
Take the flint knife,
Cut me, I dare you.

THE ROPE SEETHES[2]

2. A single noose from the Dakota hangings of December 26, 1862, has been preserved in the collection at Fort Snelling, Minnesota. In 2011, representatives from the Dakota Nation visited the collection to see the noose. Prayers were offered. For additional readings on the histories of hangings, see *The Thirteenth Turn: A History of the Noose* by Jack Shuler, 2014.

SAVAGE INDIAN FEEDS GAR WOMAN

June 1875

Bellevue Place Sanitarium, 333 S. Jefferson Street,
Batavia, Illinois

3:00 a.m. A slight breeze blows the gauzy curtains open.
Moonlight floods the room.

MARY TODD LINCOLN

Cleave unto me,
Seduce,
Fetter,
Handcuff,
Wheel clamp the irons,
Savage, I cease all protestations.

SAVAGE INDIAN

Checks her scalp for nits.
Wipes excess bear grease from his hands on her nightdress.
Fills her gaping mouth with fescue and sod.

How does it taste, Gar Woman?
You said,
"If they are hungry, let them eat grass
Or their own dung."[3]
Trader Andrew Myrick's words,

---

3. "Minnesota Indian War of 1862," Lincoln's Legacy, online exhibit, State Historical Society of North Dakota, accessed May 14, 2018, http://history
.nd.gov/lincoln/war2.html.

Lower Sioux Agency, August 15, 1862, but
Your sentiments spoken more than once.

MARY TODD LINCOLN

Swallows.

June 9, 1875.
I am in possession only of my name,
Mary Todd Lincoln, bewildered with a joy so noble
I, too, could expire.

SAVAGE INDIAN

Places her wedding ring on his little finger.

Who says Abe is dead?

LONG NIGHT'S MOON

June 1875

Bellevue Place Sanitarium, 333 S. Jefferson Street,
Batavia, Illinois

4:00 a.m. Many candles light her room. The air is hot and stifling.

SAVAGE INDIAN

*Shackles Mary Todd Lincoln to the chair for the fifty-seventh
time tonight.*

Gar Woman. That is your true name. Gar feed at night,
Sometimes eat their own eggs.

We were all once fish.
The scent of woman during copulation reminds us.

MARY TODD LINCOLN

Vulgarity at last, just like my Mr. L.
He once asked me, why is a woman like a barrel?

SAVAGE INDIAN

Shrugs.

MARY TODD LINCOLN

Giggles.

You have to raise the hoops before you put the head in.

SAVAGE INDIAN

*Breathes deeply through his nose. Snorts the bad air. Leaves her
side and walks around her bedroom.*

MARY TODD LINCOLN

Fiend, he was my lover, father, and comedian.

SAVAGE INDIAN

Sniffles and pinches her things.
The nit comb on her bureau intrigues him the most.

Fishy in here.

MARY TODD LINCOLN

Smooths the wrinkles of her sour nightdress, the one she's worn
since March 12, 1875.

Ghoul, specter, poltergeist, banshee,
You are the fishy one.
Savage, be gone from my head!

SAVAGE INDIAN

Quiet, someone is coming.

MARY TODD LINCOLN

No doubt the Wandering Jew,
Nightly he steals my pocketbook.[4]

SAVAGE INDIAN

Woman, be still!

---

4. Mark E. Neely Jr. and R. Gerald McMurtry, *The Insanity File: The Case of Mary Todd Lincoln* (Carbondale, IL: Southern Illinois University Press, 1986), 7.

He moves in close, gently caresses her face. Takes the smallest sharp flint from his leather pouch, slits the soft skin above each eyelid, sews it firmly open with a thread of silver filigree, then cuts out her left cheekbone.

MARY TODD LINCOLN
Ecstatic.

Oh! At last I can see the world as it truly is.

THE ROPE SEETHES

NOW I LAY ME DOWN

June 1875

Bellevue Place Sanitarium, 333 S. Jefferson Street,
Batavia, Illinois

4:00 a.m. She sits in a chair in her bedroom. A small candle
blooms on the bureau.

MARY TODD LINCOLN

Tattoos adorn his arms and hands.
Like night-blooming cereus, they prick the skin, slash
my will.
The savage says nit-picking takes time and patience but
can be very
Enjoyable for both parties.

SAVAGE INDIAN
Combs her oily hair.

Immerse any nits or lice in kerosene.
Pull them from the hair; drop in bowl;
Pin the cleaned sections of hair aside,
Scissor-divided segments close to the scalp. Wait.

MARY TODD LINCOLN

These many days after dear Abraham, I have come
to this,
Hairless with a deformed cheek,
Those of us with eyes sewn open
Perceive nothing to fear,

Not
Gunpowder, walls afire,
A wild Dakota Indian,
The Presidential Box at Ford's Theatre,
A hangman's noose.

SAVAGE INDIAN

Silence, Gar Woman!

Ever so gently he takes two sharp flints from his leather pouch and examines them and chooses the smallest. He approaches her face with determination. They assent to their nightly ritual, the one she craves.

MARY TODD LINCOLN

Picks up the mirror and studies her face.
Her thin upper lip curls into a smile.

I faint from the ecstasy.

THE ROPE SEETHES

THE ROPE

Out of Fort Snelling's coffin,
I swing like a fool on holiday
Backward, forward, and
Around and around.

Artwork of The Rope found at Fort Snelling

THE ROPE SPEAKS

July 4, 1875

Bellevue Place Sanitarium, 333 S. Jefferson Street,
Batavia, Illinois

The Rope hangs from the ceiling in Mary Todd Lincoln's sitting room.

THE ROPE

I done it.
Done 'em all.
I come when I'm called
Like a dog,
A horse,
A lover.

This is how I make brothers and sisters.

THE ROPE

Begins to fashion a second noose with his hands.

Start with a piece of string or rope three feet in length.

Bring one end of the loop down parallel to the original rope and fold it into thirds. It should form a wide sideways S. The lead (the left side) should be left longer so that you have some string left at the end for tying to something.

With the bottom of the original C, wrap the end of the rope around the loop several times, from the bottom near your hand, upward.

With the rope that has been wound around the *C*, poke the end of the rope through the top of the loop left by the *S*.

Once the loop is fully tightened, the task is complete.

THE ROPE

Laughs. Holds up the noose for inspection.
Hangs it from a rafter in Mary's bedroom.

A good noose should have one giant loop at one end and a piece of rope at the other end.

Artwork of two hangman's nooses

THE ROPE SEETHES

THE ROPE

Two down, thirty-six more to go.

Artwork of Mary Todd Lincoln and
Savage Indian admiring The Rope's creations

SAVAGE INDIAN LAMENTS

July 4, 1875
Bellevue Place Sanitarium, 333 S. Jefferson Street,
Batavia, Illinois

Savage Indian walks amid all the clutter in her sitting room.
Mary Todd Lincoln paces.

SAVAGE INDIAN

I know isolation.
Silence.
The slow descent downward,
Lost somewhere in midair.

Gar Woman, I have crippling doubts, but
I surrender nothing, not even in death.

He looks at their surroundings.

I no longer have to worry.
That doesn't mean I am not suspicious of the living.
They enter my dreams uninvited.

In Dakhóta land, they are pulling down the last of our dead,
Bodies of men and women hanged by a rope of lies.

When I was a human being,
I would sing the air thick with Dakhóta songs.

December 26, 1862.
In one hundred and fifty years, the citizens of Mankato
will shiver,

Asking why their ancestors hanged thirty-eight Dakhóta
Indians over a
Handful of hens' eggs.

When I look at your world, I weep
Because in the end, even your life is a captivity account.
Maybe we are all captives of one sort or the other.

He stops and drinks water from her china teacup.

For the thirty-eight lives abandoned.

In that moment in Mankato, I was misplaced.
Maybe the Nightjars carried my spirit to safety,
Back to the beginning even before Mother Earth existed.
You are probably wondering when. What millennium?
Because in your eyes every hour is measured.

To die alone while dying with thirty-seven others.

This is where I tell you about my friend's dying.
A death song, he sang it, then we sang together.
On the platform in Mankato, we tried to grasp hands,
shouting to the winds,
Mni Sóta Maḳoce, land where the waters reflect the skies,
The land where we die.
Words caught in our throats. Choked by a muscular rope.

Savage Indian raises the teacup again to salute The Rope.

Rope, he held fast.

The Rope takes a bow.

Eighteen sixty-two, almost like a birthday.
Tiny needles sew shut the muslin cloth around our faces.
Buried in a mass grave only to be dug up,
Stolen by physicians to be used as medical cadavers,
Later stored in cast-iron pots.

Still,
Our bodies cramped and squirmed in the wind, our
spirits scattered.
All of us, Gar Woman, still hang,
And you, dressed in a stinking nightshift,
The one you refuse to remove all these months,
Can never cover the past.

The soldiers are pulling on their boots,
They are not the ones they think they are.

When I am myself as I am tonight, every word is a weapon.
When I am myself as I am tonight, why can't I forget what
happened and
Take you amid the dried-up tingling in my head,
The dried-up prickle between my legs,
The ravaged filaments of desire.

Oh, I lied to settlers, I lied to preachers,
But Gar Woman, you are not who you claim to be,
You bring a child into the world and intensely regret it,
Despite your theatrical tears for pity when another son dies.

You believe you know what must be done with your
Brews and tainted teas.

But I have seen the ghosts of Abraham, Eddie, Willie,
even Tad,
Shrink when you enter a room,
Shadows escaping your burning sun.

What happens next, Gar Woman?
You've swallowed all but one of your eggs.

*Savage Indian grabs Mary Todd Lincoln by her shoulders and
pulls her to him.*

Because the wind refuses your touch
Because the insects abandoned the ground where you sleep
Because your prayers wilt the prairie grasses
Because at dawn every breath is a trial
Because with your eyes sewn open you still see nothing

Because everything you touch leaves a bruise.

The muskets are being reloaded
The carbines are being reloaded
The large-bore rifles are being reloaded
The Gatling guns are being reloaded
Emancipate me.

Fire!

THE ROPE SEETHES

THE ROPE

And now a bloody red tongue unspools.

Scene 2

A House Divided

SAVAGE INDIAN DREAMS

July 1875

Bellevue Place Sanitarium, 333 S. Jefferson Street,
Batavia, Illinois

9:00 p.m. Savage Indian watches the moonrise from the window-sill of Mary Todd Lincoln's sitting room.

SAVAGE INDIAN

Yellow buds
Green grass
Wind buds
Prairie grass
She,
Woman Who Strokes My Face,
Her gentle moans

Sweetgrass nights
Water grass
Watching butterflies course
Autumn winds
Wild turnips
Buffalo robe
Home

Wakan Tanka
Wakan Tanka
Wakan Tanka
Wakan Tanka

When will I wake?

SUNDAY LAUNDRY

July 1875

Bellevue Place Sanitarium, 333 S. Jefferson Street,
Batavia, Illinois

Dawn.

MARY TODD LINCOLN

On occasion I still go after your laundry.
Taking them in my arms,
I ravage them one by one,
A stained débardeur, the one you treasured,
An Irish linen handkerchief you carried to that dreadful
house,[5]
The squeaking black shoes, made specially for you, rarely
worn,
You claimed they pinched your toes.
No, I did not sell all of your things.
Gracious, the lies they tell about me.

On occasion I walk the landscape of your smells,
Your crop of thick hair and full lips,
The aftertaste you once left in my mouth.
Your lucky nightshirt, the one you wrote in,
And I dared not interrupt you, remember.
Burying my nose in your armpits,

---

5. She referred to Ford's Theatre as "that dreadful house." W. Emerson Reck,
A. Lincoln: His Last 24 Hours (Columbia, SC: University of South Carolina
Press, 1994), 160.

I inhale deeply and grab myself . . . down there.
Rub to pleasure. *Oh . . . oh.*
As always, this must do.

FIRST CUT

July 1875

Bellevue Place Sanitarium, 333 S. Jefferson Street,
Batavia, Illinois

Mary Todd Lincoln's bedroom at Bellevue Place.

MARY TODD LINCOLN
Stares into her handheld mirror.

You ask, dear Reverend Ward, why blood drips
From the cuff of my dress sleeve?

A wild savage cut me, sir.

SAVAGE INDIAN
Looks up from reading the newspaper.
Liar.

MARY TODD LINCOLN
Playfully sticks out her tongue at Savage Indian.

I assure you, Reverend Ward, the wild Indian came out
of nowhere.
He gave chase across the school ground,
I could feel the beast's hot breath on my neck.
He felled me.
I wrestled with the demon just as Jacob did at the river
Jabbok.[6]

---

6. Genesis 32:22–32 (New Revised Standard Version).

Savage Indian opens his leather pouch and examines his flints.

MARY TODD LINCOLN
Lays the mirror aside. Paces the room.

First cut.
Shelby Female Academy in Kentucky,
Nine years a second home,
More's the pity, Reverend Ward shamed me,
Called me precocious.
"You are not Jacob," he said. "Jacob was Israel renamed
'He who wrestled with God.'
Do not claim this for yourself."

She cries.

Oh how I wept for Mother,
Often. Abandoned by Father, a man I barely knew.
When I felt nothing,
I used a kitchen knife.

Pauses.

My house is again broken,
Rotting in a dredge rain.
Savage, give me a sharp blade,
I'll show you what a knife can do.

Mary Todd Lincoln pushes up her sleeve, exposing old wounds.

*Savage Indian moves toward her. A drum pounds as he cuts
Mary Todd Lincoln's eyelids. With careful precision, he takes her
scalp, holds it high in the air like a trophy, chanting a warrior's*

call. The drumming continues as he dances around the room, completing their nightly assent.

MARY TODD LINCOLN
Crawls quickly on her hands and knees.
Retrieves her hand mirror. Admires her image.

Oh yes, yes, Reverend Ward. The wild Indian scalped me.

Look at me when I am talking to you!

SAVAGE INDIAN IMAGINES
MARY TODD LINCOLN

July 1875

Bellevue Place Sanitarium, 333 S. Jefferson Street,
Batavia, Illinois

All is quiet. Savage Indian sits at Mary Todd Lincoln's desk,
studies her accounts.

SAVAGE INDIAN

Her light, a blush of shame.

MARY TODD LINCOLN SINGS
A LOVE SONG

August 1875

Bellevue Place Sanitarium, 333 S. Jefferson Street,
Batavia, Illinois

8:00 p.m. Dusk. Twenty-three candles blaze atop the piano,
signifying the years she was married to Abraham Lincoln. The
air stifles. She plays and sings.
Savage Indian stands next to the piano.
The Rope swings from the rafters in Mary Todd Lincoln's room.

MARY TODD LINCOLN

"And since you leave me
And thus deceive me
No scene can give me
Relief from pain
My only lover
Has prov'd a rover.
All joy is over.

My tears are vain."

SAVAGE INDIAN

Another séance, Mary? What news of the Dakhóta?

MARY TODD LINCOLN

Sings.

"Then go forever, dear Abraham,
Yet though we sever

Alas I never
Can wish you ill."[7]

*She stops playing, dabs her eyes with her handkerchief, and looks
up at Savage Indian.*

Matilda again, always her.
You didn't know Mr. Lincoln
Had a love—before me?
She was indeed more beautiful.

Now I alone remember her as he did.
Her mouth of envy,
Perfect teeth flashing like a viper, blinding all reason,
I prayed her light would burn out of plague,

But I won him,
Using my mouth.
I swallowed him!

SAVAGE INDIAN
Shows his surprise.

MARY TODD LINCOLN
What? I couldn't risk gravidity.

She continues playing.

---

7. Mrs. Alsop (lyricist) and A. Clifton (arranger), "And Since You Leave Me,"
(Baltimore: G. Willig's Music Store, 1824), accessed May 14, 2018, http://
www.pdmusic.org/1800s/24asylm.txt.

Artwork of Mary Todd Lincoln's hands,
up close, making her own noose

THE ROPE SEARCHES FOR HIS LEGACY

August 1875
Bellevue Place Sanitarium, 333 S. Jefferson Street,
Batavia, Illinois

THE ROPE

I know the secret thrill of taut,
Tying up, tying down,
Binding tight,
Strapping hard,
Lashing knot to payload—*for kicks,*
I am a collar,
A strangler,
I float in the wind like a flag on holidays.

I inspire national pride.

SAVAGE INDIAN, ALL MY RELATIONS

September 1875
Bellevue Place Sanitarium, 333 S. Jefferson Street,
Batavia, Illinois

*11:00 a.m. Lincoln's catafalque floats into Mary's rooms on a
pocket of air. Savage Indian lies inside a coffin on the same
platform President Abraham Lincoln did on April 19, 1865.*

SAVAGE INDIAN

Behold. I am what I was,
Dakhóta.
I am what I will be,
Dakhóta.
My words this night vibrate from the past to
Future constellations.

Ten million Natives in the New World in 1492.
Nine million Natives dead by 1860.
Thirty-eight Dakhóta hanged December 26, 1862.
Two hundred thousand Natives surviving in 1890.
Five million Natives alive in the New World in 2010.

Our seven council fires burn undaunted.
We live.
We live.
We live.
We live.

MARY TODD LINCOLN

Peers inside the coffin.

You are all Mr. Lincoln to me.

THE ROPE SEETHES

Another noose hangs from the rafters in Mary Todd Lincoln's suite.
Then another.
Another.
Another.
And another.

THE ROPE

We're making progress here.

MARY TODD LINCOLN, SUMMER MANIC LIGHT

September 1875

Bellevue Place Sanitarium, 333 S. Jefferson Street,

Batavia, Illinois

4:00 p.m. The light is golden. Mary sits at her desk writing letter after letter, pleading for her release.

SAVAGE INDIAN

Reads aloud from the Chicago Tribune. *Laughs.*

Warning, Cigar Thief Indian Stalks Supply Wagons.

MARY TODD LINCOLN

Moves her arm slowly across her paper.

At some point in your life, you realize that no one will ever touch you again

Or hold you in that special way your finest lover once held you—fingering the

Swollen flower between your legs, gently forcing it open; and you respond to the

Gesture so willingly wet, squeezing the third finger again and again; your breath

Entering a hungry, unrefined mouth; when his stamen finally pierces,

You cry out unexpectedly, even weep, knowing this touching to be the false

Promise of matrimony.

Did you know he once saved the strands of my hair, the ones that fell from my

Brush, saying they gave him a certain kind of pleasure?
The longest hairs, he saved in his desk drawer.

SAVAGE INDIAN
Puts the newspaper aside.
It's the same for us when we take a head of hair from an
enemy.

MARY TODD LINCOLN
He never kept the strands of Matilda's hair as he did mine.
He never loved her!

Pauses.

But at some point in your life, you realize that no one will
ever touch you again.
That way.

She pulls a loose blue thread from her dress sleeve.

Later, of course, he was shot.

And so you choose relief, a cup of special tea, a dose or
two of laudanum. Tiptoeing on squeaky floors can be
costly, though. Once, I fell on my backside and laughed
so hard I woke the corners of every room. A servant
finally came running . . .

SAVAGE INDIAN
Yawns.
Bad medicine.

MARY TODD LINCOLN

Best medicine, fool! With laudanum I could rest easy.
Oh how I tried to make life
The same for those bestowed on me. Laudanum, I used for
the children's weak
Lungs—and mine. It suppresses coughs.
The Todds are renowned for having weak lungs.

SAVAGE INDIAN

The Todd men are renowned for their drunken brawls and
brutality.

MARY TODD LINCOLN

My dear sons, all succumbed now, save Robert Todd Lincoln.

SAVAGE INDIAN

The clever one.

MARY TODD LINCOLN

The same.

SAVAGE INDIAN

An indifferent moon rises tonight. Good for memories,
good for telling stories.

MARY TODD LINCOLN

Perhaps the new one will not live. I said that to my dear
Mr. Lincoln shortly

Before Robert was born. "Molly, Molly," he said with his head in his hands.
Then he left my bed.

SAVAGE INDIAN
Folds the newspaper.

MARY TODD LINCOLN
Did you know when I left the White House after Mr. Lincoln was buried, not a
Single soul clasped my hands to bid me farewell or express sorrow for my fate.
It was as if I were dead and buried with the president.

Will no one ever touch me again?

SAVAGE INDIAN
I will.

He offers his hand to her, and together they twirl around the room to a waltz that is playing on the piano, sans pianist. A Dakota drum can be heard over the waltz.

SAVAGE INDIAN
In this dream I live.

Artwork of Mary's room with the piano at Bellevue Place Sanitarium

MARY TODD LINCOLN LOVE SONG

September 1875
Bellevue Place Sanitarium, 333 S. Jefferson Street,
Batavia, Illinois

MARY TODD LINCOLN

Sits at the piano.

"And since you leave me
And thus deceive me
No scene can give me
Relief from pain
My only lover
Has prov'd a rover.
All joy is over.

My tears are vain."

Stops playing.

My husband's spirit tells me that in the future,
Metropolitan police of the district
Will shoot black men
And black children on
The streets of Washington like moving targets.
A homeless beggar with a dog is shot dead.
A black man named Gurley will be shot dead

In a dark stairwell of New York City public housing.[8]
Who says Northern abolitionists accept Negros?

SAVAGE INDIAN

Another séance, Mary? What news of the Dakhóta?

MARY TODD LINCOLN

Sings.

"Then go forever
Yet though we sever
Alas I never
Can wish you ill

While life is dearest
And joy is nearest
Thou Pinkie dearest
I love thee still.

My tears are vain."

Stops playing.

Hear me, Pinkie,
You're not the only man
Violated for his race.

---

8. Sarah Maslin Nir, "Officer Peter Liang Convicted in Fatal Shooting of Akai Gurley in Brooklyn," *New York Times,* February 11, 2016, https://www .nytimes.com/2016/02/12/nyregion/officer-peter-liang-convicted-in-fatal -shooting-of-akai-gurley-in-brooklyn.html.

SAVAGE INDIAN
Walks toward her.

I am not Pinkie.

MARY TODD LINCOLN
Sings between fits of crying.

"My tears are vain.
In a thousand years,
A breath in the future,
A distant dream."

Oh, Pinkie, what will we keep?
What will we lose?

SAVAGE INDIAN

Pinkie was a little Indian maid you conjured
During a séance with
Your husband and friends.
I AM NOT PINKIE![9]

He grabs her, binds her legs and arms.

MARY TODD LINCOLN
Coos with pleasure.

Such pageantry I've missed since Mr. Lincoln's demise.

---

9. Mark E. Neely Jr. and R. Gerald McMurtry, *The Insanity File: The Case of Mary Todd Lincoln* (Carbondale, IL: Southern Illinois University Press, 1986), 81.

MARY TODD LINCOLN IMAGINES SERENITY

September 1875
Bellevue Place Sanitarium, 333 S. Jefferson Street,
Batavia, Illinois

MARY TODD LINCOLN

Looks kindly at Savage Indian as he sleeps in his chair.

One breath fills the teapot,
One breath pours.
Tonight, your flint knife stumbles and draws conclusions.
Here, we languish in a room filled with betrayal,
And the strangeness of being alone with you, and yet,
still alone.

THE ROPE SEETHES

THE ROPE

Three cat fits, and one duck fit to come.

MARY TODD LINCOLN, MEET THE RELATIVES

September 1875
Bellevue Place Sanitarium, 333 S. Jefferson Street,
Batavia, Illinois

11:00 a.m. Outside on the grounds of the sanitarium. Mary hasn't slept in days. Regularly she puts her hands over her ears to block the noise in her head. Savage Indian watches her from a dark corner of the room.

MARY TODD LINCOLN

Betwixt rage and sorrow, I to and fro.

She gathers stems and white flowers of the snakeroot.

Robert Todd Lincoln, you monstrous man!
My boy-you, what has happened to the babe I nourished?
You've grown secretive, cruel as Janus.
Lookie what I found growing on the estate grounds
As if a flower, a pretty bloom, *Ageratina altissima.*
Its poison remains active even after the plant dries.
White snakeroot induces milk sickness and so much more.
Did you know, my boy-you,
Ageratina altissima killed Nancy Hanks Lincoln?
Your father's mother. Your grandmother.
Country woman, poor thing. Obtuse.
Most likely illegitimate. Didn't know a thing about plants.
Tell me, Robert, is there a God that can stop me from
killing—
My boy-you?

I would like to skin you like a fetid fish,

Feed your conscience to worms,

Poor creatures, they would starve on so thin a meal.

I remember all, how you looked suckling at my breast,

Cross-eyed.

God bent one eye in, the other out.

"A warning," said Emilie, my dearest younger sister.

"Cast of the eye," said Lizzie, my older sister,

A bad sign.

I would have none of it. I coddled, cooed, and persuaded
with kisses

Your sweet eyes to focus.

As they once only beheld the image of me.

Betrayer. I will not be lulled, silenced, nor survived by my
boy-you.

MARY TODD LINCOLN PLANS AN ESCAPE

September 1875
Bellevue Place Sanitarium, 333 S. Jefferson Street,
Batavia, Illinois

A nurse forces Mary Todd Lincoln back into her bedroom. She pours a glass of water for Mary and places it on the bedside table and then leaves. Mary retrieves a bowl of plant matter from beneath her bed. She stirs the water into the mixture. Covers it with a dry cloth. Slips it under the bed next to a chamber pot filled with human wreckage.

MARY TODD LINCOLN

Now it must steep.
Soon, Robert dear, we will take tea together.
When breath shortens to choking fits,
Hardening at last my will,
Burning my lungs,
And goes on burning,
Breaking bone from sinew,
Shattering the connection between us,
You will see at last
Our world indeed is a bitter gasp.

In this dream we die.

SAVAGE INDIAN CLEANS HOUSE

September 1875
Bellevue Place Sanitarium, 333 S. Jefferson Street,
Batavia, Illinois

*Savage Indian enters the room and retrieves the bowl of plant
mixture from beneath her bed.*

SAVAGE INDIAN

She's found the laudanum again.

*He tosses the plant mixture out the window,
Accidentally killing Nightjars,
A wandering skunk,
Two field mice.
Even the grass wilts in sorrow.*

SAVAGE INDIAN AT PRAY

September 1875

Bellevue Place Sanitarium, 333 S. Jefferson Street,

Batavia, Illinois

Midnight. Savage Indian builds a fire on the grounds of Bellevue
Place Sanitarium. He smokes his pipe and prays for the dead
Nightjars, prays for the dead skunk, prays for the two dead field
mice and the wilted grass.

SAVAGE INDIAN DREAMS OF GOATS

September 1875
Bellevue Place Sanitarium, 333 S. Jefferson Street,
Batavia, Illinois

SAVAGE INDIAN

Opens Mary Todd Lincoln's trunks, searching for laudanum.

Collecting and hoarding,
Traits of the federal Indian agents.

He reads aloud from a faded sheet of paper.

October 1, 1872. Bill of lading. Mary Todd Lincoln.
Three watches, $450.00; jewelry, $700.00; soaps and
perfumes, $200.00; seventeen pairs of gloves, $60.00; three
dozen handkerchiefs, ribbons, curtains, and sashes, $300.00.

He finds a new dress in a trunk. Puts it on over his clothes.

MARY TODD LINCOLN

Watches him from her chair.

Our last child is thoroughly slicked dead, I know.
I combed Tad's coffin locks with my own hairbrush,
Cleaned immigrant fibers from his head,
Removed any tangles, oiling his sweet scalp,
A final act of love from a mother to her son.

SAVAGE INDIAN

Holds up a lace bodice. Fastens it over the dress, backward.

What of Tad's goats?

MARY TODD LINCOLN

Nanny and Nanko?

Oh, dead long ago. Eaten most likely.

*She walks over to Savage Indian and unfastens the bodice and
puts it away.*

SAVAGE INDIAN

Picks up Mary Todd Lincoln's Bible and reads.
In the name of the Lord thy God, amen.

MARY TODD LINCOLN

Once, Nanny ate all the red rose bushes at the Old
Soldiers' Home, the asylum for
Disabled veterans. My Mr. L. spent one-quarter of his
presidency there.
He no longer slept in my bed, allowing that it was too
dangerous for me
And the children.

*She takes a small 9-mm revolver from the pocket of her dress.
Examines it. Stands and aims at her bed.*

SAVAGE INDIAN

Thou shalt not kill.

MARY TODD LINCOLN

Just Mr. Lincoln and the goats
And his soldiers sleeping together in their cozy sanctuary

Away from the heat of Washington,
Away from me, where he could dream of Matilda.
Did you know he once called her name in my bed?

SAVAGE INDIAN

Thou shalt not commit adultery.

Pauses.

MARY TODD LINCOLN

Nanko chewed the bulbs planted by John Watt,
Our White House gardener.
Mr. Watt and his wife were such good friends.
They helped me earn a little extra money, too.

Wistfully.

Dr. Patterson came by this morning to examine me?
He said I must forgive Robert Todd Lincoln
For condemning me to the nuthouse.
For stealing my fortune.

My oldest son and only survivor.

There is a bitter hollow left in my heart by what
Robert's motivations provide me,
In this asylum,
In this house of foulest deeds.

She points the revolver at Savage Indian.

Peculiar that our children must outsurvive us,

Like thieves in the house, they take all,
Even a body's milk. Bone. And blood.

SAVAGE INDIAN

Abstain from all appearance of evil.

MARY TODD LINCOLN

So my actions astound you?

SAVAGE INDIAN

You've killed before.

MARY TODD LINCOLN

Quotes Shakespeare.

"What are these,
So wither'd and so wild in their attire,
That look not like the inhabitants o' the earth,
And yet are on't? Live you? Or are you aught
That man may question? . . .
By each at once her choppy finger laying
Upon her skinny lips. You should be women,
And yet your beards forbid me to interpret
That you are so."[10]

SAVAGE INDIAN

Quotes Shakespeare.

---

10. Shakespeare, *Macbeth,* 1.3.40–48, http://www.shakespeare-online.com
/plays/macbethscenes.html.

"Prithee, Kate, let's stand aside and see the end of
This controversy."[11]

MARY TODD LINCOLN

Holds her head as she paces around the room.

Quiet, Savage!
I intend to shoot Robert Todd Lincoln with Tad's revolver.
Mr. Lincoln and I gave Tad the gun. Mine now.
Call this escapism if you like. Or you can think of it as
revenge.

SAVAGE INDIAN

Reads from the Bible.

Thou shalt not kill.

MARY TODD LINCOLN

Grabbing her ears screaming.

Stop speaking! You cannot read the Bible or quote
Shakespeare.

SAVAGE INDIAN

If the doctor is adroit, convenable,
And says "I am all in your head,"
Then, dear lady, regrettably,
I know what you know.

---

11. Shakespeare, *The Taming of the Shrew,* 5.1.49–50. http://www.shakespeare
-online.com/plays/tamingscenes.html.

But the truth is I read because a white man at Fort Snelling
Taught me to read the Bible.
He also quoted long passages of Shakespeare's plays,
Marvelous stories.

Some Dakhótas took a sensible course and began to live
like white men.
There was good reason for this,
But look what happened. My hair was clipped by the
Indian agent in 1859.
And I was still hanged with my short hair in 1862.

MARY TODD LINCOLN

You were hanged because you are a killer.
And take off my clothes, fiend. They're mine.
Everything here belongs to me.

SAVAGE INDIAN

In the name of the Lord thy God, amen.

MARY TODD LINCOLN

Do not pray for me, Savage!
I have suffered for my convictions,
Suffered the poor,
Suffered the slaves,
Suffered my children,
Suffered my husband's love of another woman,
And now I suffer a vicious red man.

Don't you know?
I was the STAUNCH ABOLITIONIST in the Todd clan,
More committed to freedom than the God of Abraham,
More committed to freeing the slaves than the radical
wing of the
Republican delegation.

Fools. They created only monsters.
And to think I was Mr. Lincoln's literary editor.

Now here I am imprisoned in an asylum,
My eyes cracking like egg yolks,
Nightly my face tortured,
My blood glows red hot through crisscrossed wires
While Negros enjoy their freedom.

SAVAGE INDIAN

Far from here, the Dakhótas enjoy freedom.

MARY TODD LINCOLN

Freedom will never be yours, not in this land.
Soon I will be absolved of this place. Free.
Unlike you, who can never escape the past,
Hanged by the neck with your brutal kinsmen.

Trust to it, in the future there will again be a rain of
sorrow for me.
Mother to the dead and dying, that's what they will say.

As for Robert Todd Lincoln, in one hundred fifty years hence,
People will say, "She never meant to hurt him."

SAVAGE INDIAN
Takes the flint from his leather pouch and slowly approaches her as if to take the gun.

Gar Woman eats her last egg.

MARY TODD LINCOLN
Nightjar's chirr at dawn while
I await my dearest and only living progeny.
Silhouetted in boneless waters,
I rise, filling my gills with air
before striking,
And if we die in this half-lurid life
Well—

She fires the gun at Savage Indian. No shot is heard at Bellevue Place, only the ghostly sounds of lurid pleasure as Savage Indian and Mary Todd Lincoln assent to their nightly ritual.

THE ROPE SEETHES

THE ROPE

A home life, at last. All we need now is a rubber plant.

SAVAGE INDIAN COUNTS HIS SORROWS

September 1875
Bellevue Place Sanitarium, 333 S. Jefferson Street,
Batavia, Illinois

SAVAGE INDIAN

She,
Woman Who Strokes My Face,
Kisses my mouth,
Her hands slide up and down my body,
Gently scratching my belly.
We laugh unaware that in six moons hence,
I will be taken captive with
Her delicious scent still hovering in my dreams.

There is only the grimmest sketch of what happened
December 26, 1862.
The lamentable wailings, an anxious white child gawking,
wringing his hands,
Hangman William Duley's tight lips as he cut each rope,[12]
His green eyes blazing,
Our red eyes popping blood,
My flesh becoming dust, my bones in a doctor's iron pot,
Only a story. I am no one's uncle, no one's father,
No one's husband.

Serving a mad woman's unearthly pleasures.

---

12. Hangman William Duley's photograph was discovered in 2015. Curt Brown, "Image found of man who hanged 38 Dakota men 153 years ago," *Star Tribune,* November 2, 2015, http://www.startribune.com/image-found -of-man-who-hanged-38-dakota-men-153-years-ago/339132231.

Scene 3

An Uneasy Union

SAVAGE INDIAN, WHAT HAS BEEN

September 1875
Bellevue Place Sanitarium, 333 S. Jefferson Street,
Batavia, Illinois

Thirty-eight nooses hang from the rafters in Mary Todd Lincoln's residence.

SAVAGE INDIAN
Sings.
"Wakantanka taku nitawa
(Great Spirit—what—you make)
Tankaya qa ota;
(Is large—and—many/much)
Malipiya kin eyahnake ca,
(Sky—the—named)
Maka kin he duowanca,
(Earth—the—that is singing)
Mniowanca sbeya wanke cin,
(Water all over [ocean] make wet / moisten)
Hena oyakihi.
(These all around.)

Xitawacin wasaka, wakan,
(Mind/thoughts—strong—powerful/holy)
On wawicaliyaye;
(For/on account of—you have created)
Woyute qa wokoyake kin,
(Food—and—clothing—the)
Woyatke ko iyacinyan,

(Drinks too/also—somewhat like)
Anpetu kin otoiyohi
(Day—the—each/every one)
Wawiyohiyaye.
(Causing to, reaching to, arriving at.)"[13]

That is how I sang it on that day.

13. I am grateful to Professor Brenda Farnell, University of Illinois at Urbana-Champaign, for her help with understanding the text of *Dakota Odowan: Dakota Hymns* in the Dakota language. John P. Williamson and Alfred L. Riggs, eds., *Dakota Odowan: Dakota Hymns.* (New York: American Tract Society, 1879), https://archive.org/details/dakotao00will.

THE ROPE SEETHES,
REMEMBERING THE DAKOTA 38

THE ROPE

First symptoms:
Flashes of light,
A hissing in the ears, like a locomotive
Rounding a tight curve,
A violent struggle, faces distorting,
Eyes bursting livid as the roots of tongues
Glottal stop the larynges.

They will *never* sing again.

Earth's gravity labors on,

Kick,
Kick,
Kick,
Kick,

I am not a judge.

MARY TODD LINCOLN ON LEAVING ASYLUMS

September 11, 1875
Mary Todd Lincoln's rooms in the home of her sister
Elizabeth Todd Edwards,
Springfield, Illinois

MARY TODD LINCOLN

Writes in her diary at her desk.
She stops and drinks from a china teacup.

Yesterday my shadow climbed out of the abyss,
Leaving behind a human ruin in the asylum at Batavia.

Today, in the bosom of my sister, I proclaim
September 11, 1875, a new beginning.
I vouchsafe September 11 to the nation that
My husband saved,
Died for.
For centuries to come, let freedom ring
On September 11,
For me and everyone, everywhere,
Amen.

THE ROPE SEETHES

THE ROPE

Ironic, they will say, she's condemned the nation on
September 11.

THE ROPE SEETHES

THE ROPE

Finally that old she-cat climbs atop her desk quick as
you please.
Yearning for an eternity box, she is.
I come when I'm called,
I'm not a doctor.
I slip around her neck, hollering,
"Jump."

SAVAGE INDIAN HEROICS

September 1875
Mary Todd Lincoln's rooms in the home of her sister
Elizabeth Todd Edwards,
Springfield, Illinois

SAVAGE INDIAN

Her neck does not break,
Her spirit is strong,
Lingers like a piano note in a well-played song,

I do not pray for you,
I do not pray for you,
I do not pray for you.

He cuts her down and holds her tenderly in his arms like a lover.

MARY TODD LINCOLN

Looks at Savage Indian.

Let us agree to not make too much of this.

*Artwork of a Dakota winter count with
the events of Mary Todd Lincoln and
Savage Indian recorded*

MARY TODD LINCOLN, CATCH AND RELEASE

June 1876

Mary Todd Lincoln's rooms in the home of her sister
Elizabeth Todd Edwards,
Springfield, Illinois

Her rooms are cluttered as before. Seventeen trunks, six carpet-bags filled with footstools, silk curtains, jewelry, seventeen pairs of kit gloves, and a few hidden vials of laudanum. She pours laudanum into a china teacup and drinks it. Then a second cup of tea also laced with laudanum.
She reads aloud her letter.

MARY TODD LINCOLN
Springfield, Ill.

My dear Mrs. Bradwell:

Your most welcome letter was received last evening and I am quickly demonstrating the pleasure it afforded me by replying at once.

God is just, retribution, must follow those who act wickedly in this life, sooner or later compensation surely awaits those who suffer unjustly, if not here, in a brighter happier world. The most villainous plot has come to a close, but on Friday morning, when the young man who perpetuated it came down to Springfield, when I looked into his face (at a slight distance you may be sure) I saw the reluctance with which he yielded up what he so ignominiously fought for, my poor pittance, as the world goes—so far as wealth is concerned—a "widow's mite," my bonds. Prayers will scarcely avail in his case I think. My heart fails me when I think of the contrast between himself and my noble glorious husband, and my precious sons, who have only "gone before" and are anxiously, I am sure, awaiting the reunion, where no more separation comes—and so I told him (Robert Todd Lincoln) he could not approach us in the other world—on account of his heartless conduct, to the wife of a man who worshipped me—as well as my blessed sons did.

This one as my beloved husband always said was so very different from the rest of us. Prided himself on his philosophical nature—not satisfied with the fortune I bequeathed him in one morning, desiring the rest, brought false charges against me. The only trouble about me, in all my sorrows and bereavements has been that my mind has always been too clear and remembrances have always been too keen, in the midst of my griefs.

As to Swett he has proved himself to be the most unmitigated scoundrel and hell will be his portion and doubtless he will have company. Never could such a creature approach my husband, who loved me so devotedly—in the other life—I have my dear friend, a very great favor to ask of yourself, your good husband & the gentleman who called with you at Batavia, the City Editor of the Times. If I were to tell you three, <u>all</u> the utterances of this man Robert Todd Lincoln you would not refrain from writing the latter person up, without a day's delay. Your pen is sharp, so is Judge Bradwell's, so is the Editor's just named, of course you would not wish your names to appear, but you will not fail me, I am sure, now is the time, have justice rendered me, my dearly loved friend, see the City Editor of the Times before the close of the day when you receive *this* letter. I have been a deeply wronged woman, by one, for whom I would have poured out, my life's blood.

R. T. L.'s imprecations against you all have been very great, only on account of your being my true friends. Do not allow a day to pass before this writing is done and forwarded in every direction. Let not his wickedness triumph. It appears there is no law for the widow—in this land, and I solemnly pledge you my word as an honorable woman, that not <u>one</u> word shall ever escape my lips—not a person in <u>this</u> house or elsewhere about any article or the probable author, that may be published. My sister Mrs. E. sat by me on Friday for about an hour and a half and in a quiet composed and I trust lady like manner I gave expression to my feelings as to sins he had committed against a broken hearted woman who had been called upon to give up all her dearly beloved ones, for the time being only—and I asked him to look upon my bleached hair—which he had entirely created caused with the past sorrowful year.

Write, fail me not, I pray you, any delay will be grievous, I assure you. So much I have to tell you. Kiss your sweet lovely daughter for me. Would to heaven, I could see you. Best regards to your husband—fail me not.

Always your most affectionate friend,

Mary Lincoln[14]

---

14. Jason Emerson, *The Madness of Mary Lincoln* (Carbondale, IL: Southern Illinois University Press, 2007), 168–170.

MARY TODD LINCOLN, A TRIBE OF GHOSTS
June 1876
Mary Todd Lincoln's rooms in the home of her sister
Elizabeth Todd Edwards,
Springfield, Illinois

Twilight. The ghosts of Abraham Lincoln, Eddie, Willie, and Tad
suddenly appear. In a state of great unhappiness, Mr. Lincoln
shakes his head at Mary Todd Lincoln.

MARY TODD LINCOLN

Willie, Taddie, sweet Eddie, and Father.

She rushes to greet her family. The children recoil in fear and
hide behind their father.
Abraham Lincoln raises his hand to halt her approach.

Mr. Lincoln? What is wrong?

The four disappear. She whimpers and returns to her writing desk.
Continues reading aloud from the last passage in her letter.

"[R. T. L.], as my beloved husband always said, was so very
different from the rest of us."[15]

SAVAGE INDIAN

Appears with The Rope. Together they read over her shoulder.
Savage Indian pulls her chair away from the desk and begins to
bind her hands and feet.

Fishy in here.

---

15. Jason Emerson, *The Madness of Mary Lincoln* (Carbondale, IL: Southern
Illinois University Press, 2007), 168–169.

MARY TODD LINCOLN

Savage, you are banished from my head these past eight
months.

Go away, I no longer need you.

SAVAGE INDIAN

Sniffs an empty laudanum vial.

Unlikely.

I see Mr. Lincoln turned you away, again.

MARY TODD LINCOLN

As long ago as Matilda.

SAVAGE INDIAN

You hate her even now.

MARY TODD LINCOLN

I may still hold a grudge, but no, I no longer hate her.

She was—

Matilda captured his imagination.

And that was that.

SAVAGE INDIAN

True.

MARY TODD LINCOLN

How would you know?

I've tried feeling pity for her.
She married a stranger on a train.
And I became the First Lady of the nation.

SAVAGE INDIAN

A divided house is never a happy one.
Did poor Mr. Lincoln guess that
You secretly hoped for a Confederate win?

MARY TODD LINCOLN

Liar.

SAVAGE INDIAN

Even as ghosts, your sons know the truth of your
convictions.

MARY TODD LINCOLN

I was an abolitionist.

SAVAGE INDIAN

And a killer of children. You drugged your sons unto
death.

MARY TODD LINCOLN
Screams.

I never harmed my children!
I doctored their weak lungs,

Gave them relief.
Taddie stopped coughing.

SAVAGE INDIAN

He stopped breathing altogether.

MARY TODD LINCOLN

So did Willie—before him.

SAVAGE INDIAN

What regret, where's the remorse?
Like a good actress you showered tears on
All you came in contact with.

MARY TODD LINCOLN

My sons had maladies. Eddie tuberculosis,
Willie typhoid fever,
Taddie had a cold that grew into pneumonia.

SAVAGE INDIAN

Yes a cold, very contagious, I understand.
But neither you nor Mr. Lincoln caught pneumonia or
tuberculosis, although
You say you lived inside their every breath. Your words.

MARY TODD LINCOLN

I did as any mother would. I made them a mixture of
laudanum, water, and

Golden syrup.
A quieter for when Willie coughed,
A relief for Tad, delirious with pain.
A remedy for which I am not on trial.

SAVAGE INDIAN

Says the bird of prey after devouring
A horde of field mice pups.
If you have no guilt,
Why conjure me to torture you?
Why not conjure John Wilkes Booth?

What you seek, Gar Woman, you can never have.

MARY TODD LINCOLN

What would that be?

SAVAGE INDIAN

The true love of your husband.

MARY TODD LINCOLN

Enraged.

I was his all-in-all—he never had Matilda as he had me.
I was his beloved Molly, child-wife.
Fool, he worshipped at my altar.

SAVAGE INDIAN

So much so he left your bed.

MARY TODD LINCOLN

No matter where he slept,
I was—

SAVAGE INDIAN

The hellcat that abandoned her kittens!
Your husband was so busy killing Indians,
He didn't notice his wife was killing his sons.

MARY TODD LINCOLN

Cries.

Savage, be gone from my head.

SAVAGE INDIAN

Hear me, woman, now and forever,
Everywhere you are, I am.

He holds a flint knife to cut her but stops.

MARY TODD LINCOLN

Do it.
Do it, I say.

SAVAGE INDIAN

First, look up.

Thirty-eight Natives hang from the rafters in her room.

MARY TODD LINCOLN

I will not see them!

SAVAGE INDIAN

Listen for your words coming to life.
"Maybe General John Pope was right," you said,
"Exterminate the Sioux," you said.
"Treat them as you would wild beasts," you said.
"Hang all the savages."

MARY TODD LINCOLN

My thoughts were never expressed.

SAVAGE INDIAN

I read your letters, the ones your son will burn in a distant
future, purifying your image for history's sake.

MARY TODD LINCOLN

The Dakota massacred white women and children.

SAVAGE INDIAN

Men, too, I agree.

MARY TODD LINCOLN

You killed innocent children!

SAVAGE INDIAN

So did you!

MARY TODD LINCOLN

I didn't.

SAVAGE INDIAN

Forces her head up.

See the legacy you and your husband bestow!

Mary Todd Lincoln studies the hanged men.

SAVAGE INDIAN

You made me your confessor.
You desire agony, Gar Woman.
You swallow addiction
And grieve and grudge all, even
Your husband, his wistful dreams of another woman.
And your sons.

The truth, say it.

Mary throws a teacup at Savage Indian.

MARY TODD LINCOLN

Never!

*She throws the saucer, a teaspoon, and items on her bureau at him.
They scuffle, and he finally subdues her.*

SAVAGE INDIAN

You wanted to punish Lincoln for dismissing your
Engagement.
You believed he loved another woman, until

You realized the death of each baby aroused his deepest
Pity.

MARY TODD LINCOLN

I didn't kill them.

SAVAGE INDIAN

For a broken engagement, you punished him unto death.

MARY TODD LINCOLN

I didn't.

SAVAGE INDIAN

You exacted pain.

What of the bribes you took from your husband's
Enemies?
The Washington salary you covertly arranged for yourself
With the help of the gardener John Watt.
What of Mr. Lincoln's annual address in 1862?
You sold his speech to Congress to the *New York Herald*[16]
So they would published it before he could give it.

What manner of wife . . .

MARY TODD LINCOLN

Hides her face in her hands.

---

16. Stephen Berry, *House of Abraham: Lincoln & The Todds, a Family Divided by War* (New York: Houghton Mifflin, 2007): 102.

A woebegone
A bedraggled Nightjar.
I would embrace all my bad deeds
If I could but see Eddie, Willie, and Taddie once more,
In this life.

SAVAGE INDIAN
The truth,
No more harm can be done
From your words.

MARY TODD LINCOLN
The truth.

I want to die.

SAVAGE INDIAN
Knocks her to the floor.
Another lie.

MARY TODD LINCOLN
Grabs a flint from his pouch, stabs him several times.
Yet he does not bleed.

SAVAGE INDIAN
A strong blow from a dying woebegone.

MARY TODD LINCOLN

Leave me, Savage, I've suffered
An absent husband, sons who craved their father,
All manner of brutality, but
I suffer you no longer.

SAVAGE INDIAN
Shakes her by the shoulders.

MARY TODD LINCOLN
Twists out of his grasp and slaps him.
Stop, fiend.

All right, all right, all right.
I needed money,
For the household, for the staff . . .
And after poor Eddie died,
There was such an outpouring of pity for his mother,
I thought . . .

She calms herself, smooths her dress.

Grief became my friend, my work.

Her voice trails off.

She stands and looks at the thirty-eight Dakota bodies.
She touches their swollen feet.

Yes, I drink laudanum-laced tea,
Laudanum dulls my memory.
I still see my dress and bloody gloves from that night.

In the future they will one day be on display in the
museum in Springfield. Alongside my husband's.
That is what people will want of me. My sacrifices.

And you,
In the future I see your feathered headdresses,
Boxes of your people's bones made ready for study.
We are a pair, you and I,
Relics to be studied.

SAVAGE INDIAN
Pensive.
Not paired.

MARY TODD LINCOLN
Indeed, paired! In the future they will be staging plays
about us.

SAVAGE INDIAN
Disgusted. Goes to the window.
I've risen and searched
The empty scaffolding in Mankato,
Heard the faint cries of the Dakhótas on the wind,
Impossible to count as stardust . . .

Mr. Lincoln and all his generals thought they could end
Our race.
Where is he now?

MARY TODD LINCOLN
Drinks from a small bottle of laudanum.
Coughs from the bitterness.

Where are you?
On a dusty museum shelf,
Next to the mummy-cat.
Forgotten.

I take heart that in the future, Grand Army of the
Republic will be sent to
Clean up what pitiful lands you have left.

SAVAGE INDIAN
Hears a Dakhóta drumbeat.

Another lie!
But Robert Todd Lincoln of Manchester, Vermont,
A man in his eighties, ever his father's son,
Will burn your most odious letters
And their soured opinions,
Shielding your opium habits
From the public.
Your motherly abuse,
This I have seen.

MARY TODD LINCOLN
She holds a mirror in her hand.

I told you, we are a pair.
Abused. Abuser.

Now, I beg you.

SAVAGE INDIAN

He turns from the window. Takes his time. Scalps her. Slits her left eyelid, then her right eyelid, sews the flesh above both eyes open with wire.

Observe, Gar Woman.

She stares in the mirror.

MARY TODD LINCOLN

Breathless.

"Madness overcame her," they will say.
"Such a pity," they will say, "she had to flee to Pau, France."

SAVAGE INDIAN

Hair taken, face deformed with your eyes hooked open . . .

MARY TODD LINCOLN

I have been touched by God.

Turns to Savage Indian.

Again, please.

THE ROPE SEETHES

THE ROPE

Yes.

.

NOTES

I still remember my surprise when reading *The Insanity File: The Case of Mary Todd Lincoln* by Mark E. Neely Jr. and R. Gerald McMurtry (1986). I'd recently visited the Abraham Lincoln Presidential Library and Museum in Springfield, Illinois, and purchased a few books, including *The Insanity File*. I was reading along when the words "attributed the fiendish work inside her head to an Indian spirit" leaped off the page. Mary Todd Lincoln said an American Indian spirit was causing the anguish and pain she began experiencing each night in 1873. *Why hadn't I known this,* I wondered. At the time I was teaching at the University of Illinois at Urbana-Champaign in the American Indian Studies and English departments. Over the next seven years, I read more about Mrs. Lincoln and conferred with colleagues and friends about why she believed an American Indian was haunting her. Many books were important to my research: *The Madness of Mary Lincoln* by Jason Emerson (2007), *Mary Todd Lincoln: A Biography* by Jean H. Baker (1987), *House of Abraham: Lincoln and the Todds, a Family Divided by War* by Stephen Berry (2007), and *Lincoln's Melancholy: How Depression Challenged a President and Fueled His Greatness* by Joshua Wolf Shenk (2005). I also read local and state newspapers from the nineteenth century that helped contextualize the era in which the book is set.

I would like to thank the following people for their support, literary advice, and enthusiasm for the project: Susan

Power, John Lowe, Stephen Berry, Bao Phi, Rilla Askew, Paul Austin, Keith Cartwright, Dean Rader, Andrea Carlson, Philip Deloria, Natalie Diaz, Brenda Child, Jace Weaver, Laura Weaver, Jim Wilson, I. B. Hopkins, Marla Carlson, Magdalena Zurawski, Andrew Zawacki, and Reginald McKnight. Thanks also to the English department at the University of Georgia, Athens, where I currently teach. Finally a special thanks to Chris Fischbach for believing in the project, along with the wonderful staff of Coffee House Press.

LITERATURE
is not the same thing as
PUBLISHING

Coffee House Press began as a small letterpress operation in 1972 and has grown into an internationally renowned nonprofit publisher of literary fiction, essay, poetry, and other work that doesn't fit neatly into genre categories.

Coffee House is both a publisher and an arts organization. Through our *Books in Action* program and publications, we've become interdisciplinary collaborators and incubators for new work and audience experiences. Our vision for the future is one where a publisher is a catalyst and connector.

FUNDER ACKNOWLEDGMENTS

Coffee House Press is an internationally renowned independent book publisher and arts nonprofit based in Minneapolis, MN; through its literary publications and *Books in Action* program, Coffee House acts as a catalyst and connector—between authors and readers, ideas and resources, creativity and community, inspiration and action.

Coffee House Press books are made possible through the generous support of grants and donations from corporations, state and federal grant programs, family foundations, and the many individuals who believe in the transformational power of literature. This activity is made possible by the voters of Minnesota through a Minnesota State Arts Board Operating Support grant, thanks to the legislative appropriation from the Arts and Cultural Heritage Fund. Coffee House also receives major operating support from the Amazon Literary Partnership, the Jerome Foundation, McKnight Foundation, Target Foundation, and the National Endowment for the Arts (NEA). To find out more about how NEA grants impact individuals and communities, visit www.arts.gov.

Coffee House Press receives additional support from the Elmer L. & Eleanor J. Andersen Foundation; the David & Mary Anderson Family Foundation; Bookmobile; Fredrikson & Byron, P.A.; Dorsey & Whitney LLP; the Fringe Foundation; Kenneth Koch Literary Estate; the Knight Foundation; the Matching Grant Program Fund of the Minneapolis Foundation; Mr. Pancks' Fund in memory of Graham Kimpton; the Schwab Charitable Fund; Schwegman, Lundberg & Woessner, P.A.; the U.S. Bank Foundation; and VSA Minnesota for the Metropolitan Regional Arts Council.

THE PUBLISHER'S CIRCLE OF COFFEE HOUSE PRESS

Savage Conversations was designed by
Bookmobile Design & Digital Publisher Services.
Text is set in Minion Pro.